The Treasure of Clipper Point

By Gretchen Brassington

Illustrated by Bert Jackson

Dominie Press, Inc.

Publisher: Raymond Yuen
Project Editor: John S. F. Graham
Editor: Bob Rowland
Designer: Greg DiGenti
Illustrator: Bert Jackson

Published by:

ഉ Dominie Press, Inc.

1949 Kellogg Avenue
Carlsbad, California 92008 USA

www.dominie.com

1-800-232-4570

Paperback ISBN 0-7685-1817-2
Printed in Singapore by PH Productions Pte Ltd
1 2 3 4 5 6 PH 05 04 03

Table of Contents

Chapter One
Clipper Point

"Josh?" Sam asked. He hung over the side of the top bunk.

Pippi hung his head over, too, with his ears dangling down. He barked softly.

Josh looked up from the bottom bunk. "You know you're not allowed to have that dog in bed with you," he grumbled. "Go back to sleep."

"Hey, Josh!" Sam was insistent. "Come on. We shouldn't waste one minute of this vacation. Let's go exploring, right now."

"Exploring what?" Josh mumbled. "It's six in the morning."

"I don't know. Something no one else knows about. Something we don't even know about. That's why it's called *exploring*."

Josh opened his eyes. "Sam, we come here every year. I've been all over the cove, and so have you. There's nothing around here we don't know about."

"You never know," Sam said. "There are a lot of places we've never been."

Josh knew what that meant. Some places in the cove were off-limits. Josh

had always been curious, but he never went where he wasn't supposed to go.

But the vacation had been pretty dull up until then.

"Come downstairs with me and I'll tell you what I have in mind," Sam said.

"Oh, all right," Josh said.

The boys got Pippi down from the top bunk without waking their mom and dad.

In the kitchen, Josh made some toast, and Sam spread it with chocolate fudge sauce. Sam licked his fingers when he was finished.

Josh took his toast outside into the early morning sun. "Where do you want to start exploring, Sam?"

Sam pointed to a trail that wound up to the top of a steep hill. "Up on Clipper Point!"

Josh sighed. "You know we're not

allowed up there. The cliffs are dangerous."

"We can keep away from the cliffs. Besides, it's one place we haven't been."

"Oh, all right."

They headed out to explore. Pippi shot out into the grass and ran around them.

Josh grabbed Pippi's collar as he scampered past. "Stop chasing those butterflies, Pippi! You're not supposed to eat them!"

Chapter Two
Don't Go Near the Edge

Pippi and Sam raced up the trail. Josh followed, but soon Sam was way ahead.

Pippi chased something through the long grass beside the path.

"Slow down, Sam," Josh called. "And don't let Pippi eat anything!"

Sam waved and ran on ahead.

Josh climbed until he was worn out.
The hill got steeper.

By the time he got to the top, Josh was
ready to fall down on the grass and take
a rest.

Sam was already sitting on the grass,
well away from the edge of the cliff.

"Look at the ocean from here! We're
up so high, it looks like it's frowning."
Sam laughed.

Pippi was sitting between Sam's knees,
watching two seagulls playing tag through
the air above the cliff.

One of the seagulls swooped down
and landed lightly near the top of the
cliff. Pippi leaped out from between
Sam's knees.

Sam screamed, "Pippi! Come back!"

Josh shouted, too, "Pippi! No!"

The seagull flew off, but Pippi still chased it.

Pippi yelped, and then disappeared over the edge of the cliff.

Sam ran toward the edge of the cliff.

"No, Sam," Josh gasped. "Don't go near the edge!"

"Then hold my ankles," Sam cried, and he threw himself flat on the ground at the edge of the cliff.

Josh grabbed Sam's ankles.

Sam looked over the edge, but there was no sign of Pippi in the jumble of weeds and rocks that trailed down to the ocean below.

Chapter Three
A Rattle of Stones

"**L**et me go!" Sam yelled back at Josh. "I have to get down the cliff."

"Not a chance," Josh said.

Sam lay on the grass at the top of the cliff. "I'll find you, Pippi," he said.

He looked over his shoulder. "Josh!

What's that behind you?" Josh turned
around quickly. He let go of Sam's feet
without thinking.

Sam slithered over the edge of the cliff
and began climbing down the rocks.

"Sam, no!" Josh shouted. And then
angrily, "Samuel, come back this
instant!" But Sam kept on moving.

Josh began to lower himself over the
cliff, too.

"No," Sam called up to him. "You stay there. Then you can go for help if I get stuck."

Josh watched Sam anxiously.

Sam climbed down, feeling for rocks with his feet. Then, one of the rocks gave way, and he started sliding down the cliff in a rattle of stones.

Josh's heart beat faster. Sam disappeared.

"Oof!" Josh heard, and "Ouch!"

"Are you all right?" Josh yelled. He saw Sam wave.

"I'm OK," he heard.

Josh couldn't see Sam for a long time. Then he came out of a gap in the rocks, with Pippi under his arm.

"Come back up now," Josh said. "Carefully."

"In a minute." Sam's voice blew thinly

up the cliff. He set Pippi down and then disappeared behind some brush.

"Hey!" Josh yelled. "Where are you going now?"

Josh saw Sam coming back up, this time with both Pippi and a strange-looking cloth sack.

Chapter Four
The Sack

Sam climbed up again, with Pippi under one arm, dragging the sack behind him. Each time Sam's foot slipped and sent stones rattling into the sea below, Josh held his breath.

Sam knew Josh was worried.

"I'm all right," he called up the cliff.

"Don't watch me."

"I have to," Josh answered.

As Sam neared the top, Josh leaned over and grabbed Pippi. Then he helped Sam up onto the grass. They all sat there for a moment, panting.

"There's something heavy... in the sack," Sam gasped. "Pippi found it... in a cave."

Josh opened the top and tipped the sack upside down.

Out tumbled a pile of dirty metal pieces. They were flat and round, some of them so corroded, they had holes in them. Sam looked disappointed, but Josh smiled and picked up one of the pieces of metal. He spat on it, scratched it with his fingernail, and rubbed it on his shorts.

"These look like gold coins," Josh said. "I think you've found some old pirate treasure."

Chapter Five
It's Not Easy
Having Adventures

"**W**owee!" Sam jumped up from the grass and picked up two fistfuls of coins. "We'll be able to buy a boat," he shouted. "Do you know how many caves are in these cliffs?"

The two boys heard someone calling

up the hill trail. It was their mom and dad, and they sounded angry.

Sam picked up Pippi and went to stand beside Josh.

"Do you think this pirate treasure will keep Mom and Dad from yelling at us for coming up here?" he asked in a small voice.

"No," said Josh. "And they'll say it proves we're too young to have a boat of our own, Sam."

"Do you think we'll get to keep it?" Sam asked.

"I don't think so. It should probably be in a museum somewhere. But we might get a reward from the museum for bringing it in."

Sam nodded. "I guess we'll have to put anything we get into a savings account or something."

"If Mom and Dad let us keep anything," Josh said.

"It's not easy having adventures with parents around," Sam said.